Chapter One

Duncan is a soppy dog. He looks soppy …

… acts soppy …

... and thinks soppy thoughts.

Duncan lives with a fierce old grump called Mr Hipstone.

Mr Hipstone
looks fierce …

… acts fierce …

… and probably thinks fierce (and grumpy) thoughts.

Duncan and Mr Hipstone have been together for a long time. When you see Duncan, you know that Mr Hipstone is not far away.

And when you see
Mr Hipstone,
you know
Duncan
is close by.

Some people think Mr Hipstone was something big in the city.

Some people think he's a retired pirate.

But nobody has ever asked him, because he looks so fierce.

Sometimes Mr Hipstone is forgetful. Last Thursday he forgot to buy any supper …

… and he couldn't find any money to buy food. He looked in his city suit.

He looked in his big
pirate pockets.
Nothing.
All empty.

Mr Hipstone looked down at Duncan
and said, "Arrgh!", in a fierce and
growly voice. Duncan's tail wagged. He
knew exactly what Mr Hipstone meant.

Chapter Two

That night, Duncan and Mr Hipstone went down to the river, climbed aboard their ship and sailed out of town.

Just as the sun was coming up, they reached a secret island. They dropped the anchor and rowed ashore.

Mr Hipstone looked fiercely along the beach and into the forest. He looked down at Duncan. "Arrgh!" he growled.

Sniffing and snuffling, Duncan set off at a brisk pace. After a while, he stopped and sniffed into the sand.

Mr Hipstone's fierce little eyes lit up.
"Arrgh!" he growled.

Duncan looked up at Mr Hipstone with
a sandy nose, huffed loudly,
shook his head and …

… trotted off again, nose to the ground.

An hour later, after much snuffling and
huffing, Duncan stopped. He sniffed and
snuffled and his tail wagged furiously.
He dug his paws into the sand and started
digging like a mad thing.

Mr Hipstone disappeared under
a shower of sand.
"Arrgh!" he croaked.

Mr Hipstone started digging fiercely.
Duncan disappeared under a shower of
sand.

Mr Hipstone dug deeper and deeper.

Duncan sat and watched. He yawned.

He was just settling down for a little doze, when …

Mr Hipstone's spade hit something solid.

"Arrgh!" he shouted.

"MMMM!" thought Duncan, and he licked his lips.

A moment later, Mr Hipstone held up not a treasure chest, but a huge juicy bone.

"Arrgh!" he growled, and threw the bone in the air.

Duncan's tail wagged wildly.

"ARRGH!" roared Mr Hipstone, and he grabbed at the bone, but Duncan rushed off with it, tail twirling.

"*ARRGH!*" roared Mr Hipstone again. Duncan stopped and looked back.

Chapter Three

Duncan dashed back and peered into the
hole.

"Arrgh!" growled Mr Hipstone.
Duncan sniffed suspiciously.

With Mr Hipstone holding the other
end of the bone, Duncan slowly hauled
him out.

As Duncan sat back, puffing and panting,
Mr Hipstone snatched up the bone and
raced off, shouting, "ARRGH!"

Suddenly, Mr Hipstone heard a pitiful doggy cry. He stopped and looked back.

Duncan lay on the sand with his feet in the air.

"Arrgh!" muttered Mr Hipstone, and hurried back down the hill.

Mr Hipstone looked at Duncan very closely.

Duncan opened one eye, whined, and licked Mr Hipstone's nose. "Arrgh!" growled Mr Hipstone.

Duncan opened his other eye …

… leapt to his feet, grabbed the bone,
and was off again, tail twirling madly.

"ARRGH!" roared Mr Hipstone.

Mr Hipstone followed Duncan's doggy footprints to the brow of a sandy hill.

Great showers of sand were being flung into the air.

A moment later, he saw a wonderful sight. "Arrgh!" he growled.

Duncan huffed the sand from his nose, sat back and scratched his ear. Mr Hipstone unlocked his treasure chest and was just about to say, "Arrgh!" …

... when a cannonball split the palm tree above his head.

Duncan and Mr Hipstone crept to the top of the hill.

"Arrgh!" growled Mr Hipstone.

Duncan sniffed the breeze and recognised their old enemy, Captain Rottenleg and his horrible crew. Duncan's soppy hackles rose. He growled and rushed towards the beach.

"Arrgh!" shouted Mr Hipstone. But Duncan was gone.

Chapter Four

Captain Rottenleg grinned at his horrible crew. "That's Cap'n Hipstone's ship, right enough, mates, and where he be, so be his treasure!"

A fierce, furry fireball rushed from the trees.

The horrible crew stared. Captain
Rottenleg glared at his horrible crew.
"What?" he snarled. "WHAT?"
He turned round just as …

… Duncan arrived in a fierce flurry of sand. He grabbed Captain Rottenleg by his wooden leg, and dragged him along the beach.

"Waaagh!" shouted Captain Rottenleg.
"What is it? Get it off me!"

The horrible crew charged after their captain and grabbed Duncan from all sides.

"I know you!" shouted Captain Rottenleg. "You be Cap'n Hipstone's dog! Tie him up, men!"

"Now, you scurvy hound, we'll find out how much you're worth to your beloved Captain Hipstone. You can walk the plank, aha!"

Duncan edged out along the plank, wishing he'd eaten the huge juicy bone when he'd had the chance.

Mr Hipstone stepped out from the trees. "ARRGH!" he roared and he held up the treasure chest.

Captain Rottenleg glared at Mr Hipstone. "Well, Cap'n, you must be getting old. Giving up your treasure for a dog!" He poked Mr Hipstone in the tummy with his cutlass. "Getting fat, too! Ho! Ho! Ho!"

"I'll give you two minutes to get off the island," snarled Captain Rottenleg, "and take that mutt with you!"

Chapter Five

Mr Hipstone rowed fiercely out to the
ship, the pirate's jeers ringing in his ears.
Duncan's head hung low. Mr Hipstone
had saved him but it had cost them the
treasure. No supper for them tonight!

Duncan couldn't look at Mr Hipstone, so he looked back at the island instead.

He saw the horrible crew's jeers turn to cries of rage when they broke open the treasure chest. It was empty – except for the huge juicy bone!

Suddenly, Duncan jumped to his feet, turned and looked at Mr Hipstone's big fat tummy.

"Arrgh!" growled Mr Hipstone.

On board their ship, Mr Hipstone unbuttoned his shirt and Duncan's tail wagged madly as hundreds of gold sovereigns cascaded on to the deck.

Captain Rottenleg and his horrible crew heard a distant "Arrgh!", as they saw Duncan and Mr Hipstone sailing home to the biggest and the best supper they'd ever had.

After supper, Duncan and Mr Hipstone
sat by the fire and listened to the radio.
Duncan gazed up at Mr Hipstone, and Mr
Hipstone gazed fiercely down at Duncan.

Later, when Duncan was dozing,
Mr Hipstone looked at his dog and he
reached out and scraggled Duncan's
soppy ears. Duncan's tail beat sleepily
on the fireside rug.

"Arrgh ..." growled Mr Hipstone softly.

47

Most of the time, Duncan is a soppy dog.
And most of the time, Mr Hipstone is a
fierce old grump.

But not *all* of the time!